## — Nuestras Voces —
# Wishing on a Star with Estrella

### A Diary from 2022 to 2023

by Vanessa Ramos  illustrated by Eugenia Nobati

STONE ARCH BOOKS
a capstone imprint

In loving memory of Bianca Michelle Garcia.
Your light will forever shine bright in our hearts. —V.R.

Published by Stone Arch Books, an imprint of Capstone
1710 Roe Crest Drive
North Mankato, Minnesota 56003
capstonepub.com

Copyright © 2024 by Capstone. All rights reserved. No part of this publication may be reproduced in whole or in part, or stored in a retrieval system, or transmitted in any form or by any means, electronic, mechanical, photocopying, recording, or otherwise, without written permission of the publisher.

The name of the Smithsonian Institution and the sunburst logo are
registered trademarks of the Smithsonian Institution.
For more information, please visit www.si.edu.

Library of Congress Cataloging-in-Publication Data
Names: Ramos, Vanessa (Children's author), author. | Nobati, Eugenia, illustrator. Title: Wishing on a star with Estrella : a diary from 2022 to 2023 / by Vanessa Ramos; illustrated by Eugenia Nobati. Description: North Mankato, Minnesota : Stone Arch Books, an imprint of Capstone, 2024. | Series: Nuestras voces | Audience: Ages 8-12. | Audience: Grades 4-6. | Summary: Sixth-grader Selena Estrella Herrera's family moves to El Paso to help care for her grandfather, and she tries to reinvent herself by claiming her identity as *Strella—but the project her team chooses is about the singer Selena after whom *Strella is actually named. Identifiers: LCCN 2023020989 (print) | LCCN 2023020990 (ebook) | ISBN 9781669012795 (hardcover) | ISBN 9781669012757 (paperback) | ISBN 9781669012764 (pdf) | ISBN 9781669012771 (epub) Subjects: LCSH: Mexican American families—Juvenile fiction. | Grandfathers—Juvenile fiction. | Diaries—Juvenile fiction. | Middle schools—Juvenile fiction. | Identity (Psychology)—Juvenile fiction. | El Paso (Tex.)—Juvenile fiction. | CYAC: Mexican Americans—Fiction. | Diaries—Fiction. | Middle schools—Fiction. | Schools—Fiction. | Identity—Fiction. | Grandfathers—Fiction. | El Paso (Tex.)—Fiction. | Texas—Fiction. | LCGFT: Diary fiction. Classification: LCC PZ7.1.R3658 Wi 2024 (print) | LCC PZ7.1.R3658 (ebook) | DDC 813.6 [Fic]—dc23/eng/20230530 LC record available at https://lccn.loc.gov/2023020989 LC ebook record available at https://lccn.loc.gov/2023020990

Our very special thanks to Ashley Mayor, Georgetown University, and the following at the Smithsonian's National Museum of the American Latino: Jorge Zamanillo, Director; Emily Key, Director of Education; Adrián Aldaba, Manager of Education and Public Programs; David Coronado, Senior Communications Officer; and Ranald Woodaman, Director of Exhibitions. Capstone would also like to thank the following at Smithsonian Enterprises: Paige Towler, Editorial Lead; Jill Corcoran, Senior Director, Licensed Publishing; Brigid Ferraro, Vice President, Business Development and Licensing; and Carol LeBlanc, President, Smithsonian Enterprises.

Designed by Tracy Davies

Design Elements: Shutterstock: Anna Holyph (glitter border), natnicha pinkaew09 (glitter texture), Olga_Prozorova (glitter stars), Reinhold Leitner (vintage paper)

Any additional websites and resources referenced in this book are not maintained, authorized, or sponsored by Capstone. All product and company names are trademarks™ or registered® trademarks of their respective holders.

— Nuestras Voces —

# Wishing on a Star with Estrella

## A Diary from 2022 to 2023

### Tuesday, September 6, 2022

---

Hearing my name called in front of the class is the WORST thing about middle school. Even worse than worst: I'm a new kid in a new city at a new school. I knew my old elementary school in San Antonio inside and out, but my new middle school in El Paso is a maze. It has three grades in it—6, 7, and 8. And instead of one teacher, I have *six* different teachers and *six* different classes. It feels like too much all of a sudden for someone who is not even twelve yet.

When I entered Miss Diaz's classroom for my fourth period Social Studies class, I held my books to my chest like they were a coat of armor. The desks were empty. My eyes started to burn with tears. I pulled out my schedule to see if I was in the right place.

That's when I heard, "Are you looking for Social Studies with Miss Diaz?"

I nodded and swallowed hard past the lump in my throat.

"Welcome to class! I'm Miss Diaz, and you are . . ."

"*Strella—with a star," I said. Then I went into my name speech: "My full name is actually Selena Estrella Herrera. Long story, but I go by *Strella now. I spell *Strella with a star—or you, know, the asterisk thingy—at the beginning instead of an 'E.' Because, you know, Estrella means star, and I just think it looks neat. The star is silent . . ."

I realized I was rambling, again. That's what I do. It's kind of my thing, even though my Grandpa Raul always tells me not to talk so much or laugh so loud or to, y'know, exist.

Miss Diaz smiled, and my almost-tears turned into a smile too.

I found a seat close to the front of the room and watched as Miss Diaz welcomed each and every student at the door when they finally began to arrive.

I liked Miss Diaz and her "Sí Se Puede" T-shirt.

*I can do this*, I thought to myself, translating the words. *I CAN do this*.

When the bell rang, I perked up a little. I was ready to listen to what Miss Diaz had to say—and boy, was I surprised! She didn't shout out "Selena Herrera?" like my other teachers. And she didn't ask me, "Are you named after *the* Selena?"

Maybe it was because we had already met, but she asked us to introduce ourselves to the class with our "preferred names."

It was nice to have that moment today to just be *Strella. I didn't have to worry about who or what I should be based on my first name. You see, I *am* named after THE Selena. Megastar Selena, the Queen of Tejano Music Selena: Selena Quintanilla-Pérez.

My mom is a superfan, and so was I until everyone in fifth grade started teasing me and calling me "Selena Girl." I am a bit embarrassed at how obsessed I used to be with Selena. Like, maybe I sort of thought I *was* her? Or at least a lot like her . . . but then I learned I wasn't anything like her—the hard way. More on that later.

The only good thing about being a fifth grader was that all the little kids looked up to us. In sixth grade, nobody looks up to us. They look down, and they look mean. Especially the eighth graders. But that could just be because my brother, Juan Gabriel, is one of them. (Juan Gabriel is another famous Mexican singer . . . *Parents*.)

I changed my name for a fresh start at my new school. I don't want to be Selena Girl anymore. Deep inside though, I miss Selena. I miss how much I loved her and how much she meant to me. Maybe I can find a way to celebrate her again without trying to BE her. Becoming *Strella is a start.

What else is there to tell about me?

We left our home in San Antonio. My parents, Juan Gabriel (who we call Gabbo), and I now live with Grandpa Raul in El Paso. And I'm just trying to figure out who I'm going to be in this new house and new school in this new city with my new name.

But there is something special about Miss Diaz's room. Like maybe it is okay to have questions and not answers here.

*Gah!* I'll have to tell you about Miss Diaz's announcement tomorrow. To be continued,

\*Strella

## Wednesday, September 7, 2022

So, you might be wondering where I got this notebook. Yesterday, Miss Diaz started class by saying, "Scholars, I have an announcement. I also have a gift for each of you."

A gift? Now, she had *everyone's* attention. The room began to buzz with excitement. What could Miss Diaz possibly be announcing? And why were PRESENTS involved?

Miss Diaz walked over to her desk and grabbed a notebook off a wonky stack of books.

I had never seen a notebook like this one—the cover has a black and white pattern that looks like it is ready to burst.

Miss Diaz told us we're going to participate in Texas History Day this year. The theme is Triumph and Tragedy in History.

Nerdy news is the BEST news, if you ask me, but not everyone in my class agreed.

The buzz turned into groans as students slumped in their chairs. Some were pulling at their hair and pretend-screaming like they were in a horror movie.

I thought I was the only one halfway out of my chair and brain with excitement, but I saw a girl named Brooke turn around and give a girl named Amaryllis a thumbs-up.

So, I guess there were at least three of us who were excited.

Four, if you count Miss Diaz.

Miss Diaz tried her best to get the class on board. "It'll be fun!" she promised. She said we'd create projects to enter in the state contest. And the winners of that contest would get a free trip to Washington, D.C., to present their projects at the national competition!

Then people started straightening up in their seats. We all wondered why she didn't tell us that part first! Miss Diaz said it got even better. A new museum, The National Museum of the American Latino, had recently opened its first gallery—the Molina Family Latino Gallery in Washington, D.C. The museum offered a chance to learn more about Latino history in the United States.

But there was a catch, of course. (Why is there always a "but"?) She said we'd have to work in small groups. That's when everyone groaned again.

Miss Diaz said that we'd start with our journals, which would be "multipurpose." They would hold our writing, our classwork, and our research. She flipped through her own notebook as an example for us.

Miss Diaz had added construction paper and pictures from the internet that she had printed. She had even cut up old social studies worksheets and pasted them into her notebook. She showed us her writing flowing across the pages in different colors and handwriting styles. There were doodles and even pop-ups on the pages. *How did she do that?*

Miss Diaz said she wanted us to fill up our pages with stories from our life and that there's *power* in recording our own story. She said, "My wish for you is to realize how your story is connected to the world and our history. You may even discover that you are *contributing* to history."

I wrote *Strella on the front and added some star stickers. I was ready to write.

And I am ready to get to work on History Day.

I've never been outside of Texas. I can't help but wonder what project I can make that might get me to Washington, D.C., and into that museum where I can learn more about people like me and my family and Miss Diaz and Selena and . . . the list goes on and on!

Like the Queen of Tejano Music used to say, "All I need to do is try and do the best that I can do."

*Strella

## Friday, September 9, 2022

Sometimes it's funny how words come into your life at the right time. One of the words from our vocabulary list about the History of Texas was GENERATION.

Grandpa Raul is the oldest generation in our house, then my parents, and then me and Gabbo. We have three generations all living in the same house.

You know what that means? T-R-O-U-B-L-E.

Trouble because Grandpa Raul believes we should do everything one way.

Trouble because my mom and dad sometimes think we should do things another way.

Trouble because me and Gabbo are right in the middle, and we don't know which way to go.

*Strella

## Tuesday, September 13, 2022

Here's the writing prompt we got in Miss Diaz's class today, and I have FEELINGS about it:
**Write about the history of your name.**

If you haven't already guessed it, being named after a famous Mexican American singer is A LOT. As my dad always tells me, it's not just a name, but a *legacy*. And a legacy like Selena's is hard for anyone to live up to.

Almost everything I know about Selena I learned from the movie about her life—which I've seen more times than I can count—and also the streaming series.

I will share what I know with you. But reader beware, because there is a sad part coming up.

Way back in the 1990s (I know—that was a whole different century!), a Mexican American singer named Selena was shining bright in the world of Tejano music. Tejano is not only a type of music, it's also the Spanish word for a person from Texas, like the Tejano

Queen of Music and me. I don't know if Selena called herself a *Tejana* or not, but she was proud to be Mexican American. She had beautiful bronze skin like my dad, long black hair and red lips like my mom, and was larger than life on and off stage.

Selena started performing when she was only eight years old. She had a big voice with a lot of power, and her father was shocked by her talent. That gave him the idea of creating a family band. Selena's father, Abraham, became the manager. Selena's brother played the bass guitar, and her sister was on drums. At TEN years old—a year younger than me!—Selena became the lead singer of Selena y los Dinos. (Los Dinos was named after her father's old band.) Selena wanted to sing pop music like she heard on the radio, but her father decided they should play Tejano music. It was popular in the part of Texas they were from, but there was one BIG problem. Selena's first language was English, so she had to really practice singing in Spanish.

By the time Selena was twelve, their band had

recorded their first album. They traveled all around the Southwest and Mexico in a big bus named Bertha, performing concerts.

My dad and mom met at what turned out to be Selena's LAST concert at the Houston Astrodome. The concert was in English and Spanish, and it was even on TV. More than 60,000 people were in the stadium, including my parents.

So, you might be wondering why it was Selena's last concert. That is the terrible part of the story. At age 23, Selena was shot by someone who worked for her, and she died. It was a horrible thing. Selena was so talented and so loved by her fans that she will never be forgotten.

When I was born ON Selena's birthdate many years later, my parents knew that I would be named Selena too. They knew I would be well-loved, like Selena was, and they wanted my name to have meaning.

And I loved my name . . . until last year.

Like I said before, everyone called me "Selena Girl." Yes, I talked a lot about Selena. Yes, I did wear Selena T-shirts way too often. And yes, I dressed up as Selena for Halloween. But I mostly just got light teasing until the night of THE FIFTH GRADE TALENT SHOW.

The plan was to have my dad accompany me with his guitar, and I would sing "Bidi Bidi Bom Bom," one of Selena's greatest hits.

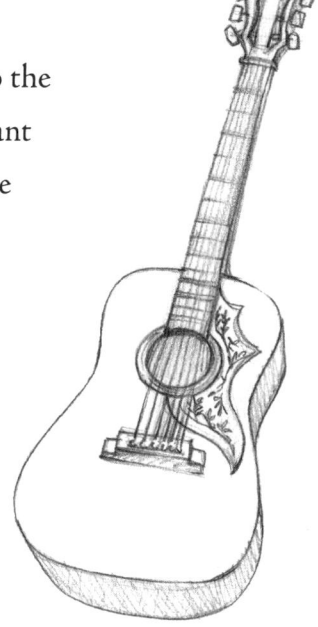

I don't want to go into the details, because I don't want my tears to smear all these words. Long story short, as I sang, a kid in the audience shouted, "Whoa, Selena Girl can't sing!" Then other students started whispering too. I felt like everyone was laughing at me. I dropped the microphone and ran off the stage. My dad followed and tried to talk to me, but I couldn't hear him over my crying. Why was I named Selena if I couldn't sing? If I could never live up to her name?

From that point on, the name Selena sort of felt like a mean joke. I didn't want anything to remind me of Selena and all the ways that I am not her.

*Strella

## Thursday, September 15, 2022

Can history be about a name that doesn't quite fit you?

Can history be about the family you belong to?

Can history help a person figure out who they are or who they want to be?

## Wednesday, September 21, 2022

You might be wondering about my familia and how we came to live with Grandpa Raul in El Paso. *Familia* means family en español, in case you don't know. Selena once said, "I didn't have the opportunity to learn Spanish when I was a girl, but it's never too late to get in touch with your roots."

This year, I'm taking Spanish, and I'm going to be all about practicing my vocabulary and getting better at speaking. Not because I overheard Grandpa Raul telling my dad that I needed to work on my Spanish. But because, like Selena, English is my first language. (Did you know Selena took Spanish lessons too?)

If only Grandpa Raul knew how much Spanish I understand—even though my palabras feel like puzzle pieces coming out of my mouth. I just can't get my Spanish words to fit together the way I can in English.

I was born in this "west Texas town of El Paso," like in some old song my dad loves to sing. But my mom, dad, brother, and I moved to San Antonio when Gabbo and I were little, so I don't remember much about living here. I think of it as Grandpa Raul's home, not ours. Not yet, anyway.

I heard Grandpa Raul once say that "The Herreras were here before Texas was Texas." So my family has been in Texas a long, long time, at least on my dad's side. My dad's name is Roy. He can play the guitar and the keyboards, and what's most amazing is that he taught himself how to do it. "By ear," he calls it, which means he can listen to almost anything and then play it. Pretty cool, right? When he met my mom, he played in a Tejano band. My dad is sensitive and smart. He works from home, so we spend a lot of time together. We both like to read and watch movies and listen to music.

Grandpa Raul is my dad's dad. All my tías and tíos call my grandpa "Father" and "Sir," maybe because he was in the army. Everyone seems to be on their tiptoes around him—even Grandma Santos when she was alive. Grandma Santos looked after Gabbo and me when we were little. I remember peeking into Grandpa Raul's library and sneaking candies from the side pocket on his recliner while he was at work. This was before Grandma Santos was sick and before her funeral, all of which turned my grouchy Grandpa Raul into even more of a thundercloud.

My mom is called Fin, short for Finola. How can I describe her? She is like a shaken bottle of soda you must open carefully. Otherwise, there's no stopping the fizzy flow of her energy. As I said earlier, my mom is the ULTIMATE Selena fan. She has CDs, magazines, newspaper clippings, old posters, T-shirts, books, and tons of other stuff. What happened to Selena was tragic, and even though it was almost thirty years ago, my mom remembers watching everything on the news. She says that without social media, the news was slower to reach people.

My mom seems to know everything. She used to work at the Guadalupe Cultural Arts Center before we moved back to El Paso. Now she's working on getting a master's degree and starting her own nonprofit.

Lastly, there is my brother, Gabbo. He is annoying and really there is nothing left to say about Mr. Eighth Grader except that he can do anything and fit in anywhere, and I don't mind telling you that sometimes I wish I could do anything and fit in anywhere too.

I don't know yet what makes me special.

\*Strella

## Thursday, September 22, 2022

I'm back! I started telling you about Mom and Dad and Gabbo, but I forgot to finish telling you how we came to live with Grandpa Raul.

School was out, and we were ready for summer! But then Mom and Dad sat us down at the kitchen table in our tiny old house in San Antonio. Mom was quiet (not normal), and Dad kept looking at his hands and wiggling his fingers as if they might make words for him.

I sat next to Gabbo and raised my eyebrows at him like, "Hey, do you know what's up?" Gabbo was never in trouble—only ever me—so why call both of us to the table? I mean I was never in *trouble* trouble. It's just that sometimes my report cards came back with good grades but also a concern about how much I liked to "socialize."

One thing you should know about me (in case you haven't noticed, Miss Diaz!) is that I do talk

A LOT. I talked so much in fifth grade that my teacher's ears used to turn red like they were going to pop off her head. When I saw that happen, I tried my best to zip my lip.

I guess this also means I write A LOT. (I hope that doesn't turn *your* ears red, Miss Diaz!)

Anyway, before I could tell my parents I would do better, I barely heard Dad whisper that Grandpa Raul was going to have heart surgery. And then he was quiet again.

That's when Mom took a deep breath and said that we were moving back to El Paso to take care of Grandpa Raul after his surgery.

"For the summer?" I asked.

"Forever," Mom said, "or at least for the foreseeable future." She said we need to be near family, and that Dad would continue to work from home, and that she was looking at "new opportunities" in El Paso.

I just kinda sat there.

Dad finally looked up and gave a small smile. He reminded us that Grandpa Raul's house is so big that we could fit our whole house inside of it. They just kept adding room after room after each one of their kids was born, and now those rooms are empty. Dad said we were going to fill up the house and fill up Grandpa's heart again.

I didn't really know what my dad meant by that. Or all the ways a person can have a broken heart.

*Strella

## Monday, September 26, 2022

Today in Social Studies, we got to choose our groups for our Texas History Day projects. (Thank you for that, Miss Diaz, because I knew I wanted to work with Brooke and Amaryllis, and they wanted to work with me too!)

We were supposed to brainstorm triumphs and tragedies in history, but we mainly talked about how super amazing it would be to travel to Washington, D.C., and also see the new museum Miss Diaz is so excited about.

(Sorry for not doing our work, Miss Diaz. Please see my last journal entry about talking and socializing too much.)

*Strella

## Wednesday, September 28, 2022

I look forward to Miss Diaz's class the most every day. She always greets us at the classroom door, and she always seems excited to be at school. Today, she gave us another writing prompt for this journal and, like always, I have a lot to say ...

**Who are you as a reader and writer? What book, story, poem, movie, song, podcast, vlog, blog, television show, etc., has most influenced or inspired you and why?**

I'm going to write about my old favorite movie,

which was—you guessed it!—*Selena*. Maybe it's still my favorite movie. I don't know. (Movie in Spanish, by the way, is *película*.) My mom said the Selena movie is a biopic, which means it's the story of a life.

So every year on April 16, which, as I mentioned, is not only *my* birthday but also Selena's birthday, we watch the movie. In Texas, April 16 is also Selena Day. George W. Bush was the Texas governor back then, and he made that declaration just two weeks after Selena's death. It's a day to remember her, and it also marks my exciting entrance into the world!

My birthday/Selena Day is always a big deal, because that's how my mom is. She hangs purple and black streamers in our dining room. She sets a dozen white roses on the table. We order a giant pizza. These were all of

Selena's favorite things, which also became all my favorite things over the years.

In the movie, Selena's dad says that the only thing more exhausting than being Mexican is being Mexican American. He says you have to be "more Mexican than the Mexicans and more American than the Americans." I think he kinda means how I feel torn between generations at Grandpa Raul's house. Grandpa Raul wants things a certain way, but that's not always how the rest of us want it. Maybe Grandpa Raul wants me to be more Mexican, whatever that means.

But I think the thing more exhausting than being a Mexican American is being named after a *famous* Mexican American who was a singer. And the only thing more exhausting than that is being born into a creative and musical family like mine when—guess what?—you have zero gifts.

ZERO. (Remember my talent show disaster?)

I don't think my family was trying to make me

into a singer like Selena. They were just sharing what they loved with me, which is music. I could show you pictures from when I was barely big enough to hold a kid-size guitar, of me and my dad at his keyboard, of me and my mom pretend-singing into hairbrushes . . . You get the idea. Music has always been part of my life, even if I'm not musical myself.

Selena didn't just love music—she also had a love for fashion. She made her own costumes and even designed her own dress for the Grammy Awards. (For the record, I don't have any fashion designer talents either.)

I think maybe I could be a writer. Maybe that comes from the music, from all these years of lyrics, which are the stories in the music. I remember my dad telling me he loved the way people sing about their pain and sometimes even their happiness.

I love the stories music can tell in between the playing and singing—how someone listening can connect to the lyrics. I want to be part of that, to record these stories of my family and give them to the world and have someone be able to say, "That's me." Even if they are not Mexican American. Even if they can't sing but are named after a famous Mexican American who could.

*Strella

## Friday, September 30, 2022

It's hard to believe I've already finished four weeks of middle school!

I'll try not to write so much today, but everything is changing faster than I can keep track of.

I really like the quiet of these pages where I can write out all the noise in my brain and then feel quiet on the inside too.

*Strella

Monday, October 3, 2022

I have been thinking a lot about the power of music and why it matters so much to my family and our culture.

I asked my dad where he thinks his love of music came from. He told me that Grandpa Raul and Grandma Santos always had people over in the backyard, and they would all sing together.

I like how his words painted a picture in my mind's eye. I can imagine everyone singing and laughing at night under the glow of the stars.

I learned that my Grandma Santos wanted to be a singer. She was born in Ciudad Juárez, Mexico.

She would sneak out of her house to go sing at the cantina! Her brothers would find her and bring her back home. They didn't think it was proper for her to be performing in public like that. Like Gabbo, her brothers were super strict.

My dad tells me Grandma sang like Lydia Mendoza. (Lydia Mendoza was a famous Mexican American singer born way, WAY before Selena.)

I don't think I've heard Lydia Mendoza's songs before, and my dad said he doesn't like to play them often because it makes him miss Grandma too much. But he said he would play some of her music for me later if I wanted.

One thing I can't picture at all is my Grandpa Raul singing. Or playing a guitar. Or being happy. My powers of imagination are not THAT strong.

## Wednesday, October 5, 2022

I remembered that I still never told you what happened over the summer. Grandpa said he would be just fine after the surgery and didn't need anyone's help. But we packed up our house in San Antonio and put it up for sale anyway.

Gabbo and I each got one big box for the things we wanted to take with us to Grandpa's. Other things were donated, sold, or put into storage.

I had to say goodbye to all my neighbors and friends, and I am not embarrassed to say how much I cried. Mom was running around here and there, trying to keep all of us organized, her fizzy energy running over. Gabbo went with the flow, like always.

It had to be the fastest move in history. My dad's goal was to get to El Paso before Grandpa Raul's surgery, and we did.

Family first is how Dad operates. I think that's how Selena's dad was too.

*Strella

## Thursday, October 6, 2022

I've been thinking about what I wrote yesterday. It reminded me of another prompt Miss Diaz gave us to write about: **What does home mean to you?** (And Miss Diaz, if I'm honest, I haven't wanted to write about this, but I will try.)

Grandpa Raul's house looked the same as it always had when we arrived from San Antonio. His library is still to the side of the kitchen and connected to a porch that leads to the backyard. When I was little, we lived in a two-bedroom trailer just outside the back door, according to my dad, but I don't remember that. The trailer isn't there anymore.

I did remember every detail of Grandpa Raul's library, though. The overflowing shelves of books, his old leather recliner, the candies in the side pocket . . .

Next to Grandpa Raul's library is a dining room and a giant rectangular living room. Down a long hallway is where bedroom after bedroom begins. I can picture the rooms being added on to the house as more and more kids were born, just as my dad described. There's also a room Grandma Santos used as a music room. This back part of the house is where my family made our own space when we moved back to El Paso.

Grandpa Raul's house may be bigger than ours was in San Antonio, but our home in San Antonio felt like we belonged to it.

I don't feel like that at Grandpa Raul's. Maybe it's because he doesn't really want us here, just like he said.

*Strella

## Monday, October 10, 2022

Miss Diaz said to look at the entries we've been making in our journals for ideas for our Texas History Day project.

When I cracked open my notebook, I was proud of all the things I had been writing. Like Miss Diaz said, we have been writing our own histories. But how can we use them for this project?

Miss Diaz told each team to make a Team Table (which is a fancy name for our desks pushed together). Today's class time was for more brainstorming. When I sat down, Brooke leaned forward and told me she'd been wanting to ask me a question. "Why do you have a star in front of your name?"

So I told her and Amaryllis everything I've shared with you so far about my name and about Selena. And of course, I also had to tell them the tragic part about how Selena died.

Both Brooke and Amaryllis stared at me with their mouths hanging open.

"*Strella, you may hate this idea, but what if we made Selena our topic for Texas History Day?"

"Yeah, she's from Texas!" Amaryllis exclaimed. "Her story fits perfectly into Triumph and Tragedy in History!"

"But maybe we could focus more on the Triumph part instead of the Tragedy," Brooke added, kindly.

I told them I wasn't sure. I was remembering being called "Selena Girl" by the kids at my old school. And about my EPIC FAIL at the talent show. I didn't tell Brooke and Amaryllis that part though.

"But your dad is a musician, and your grandma wanted to be a singer. We could interview them and find out what they know about Selena," Brooke said.

I told them that my grandma wasn't here anymore but that my dad would be happy to help.

My brain was starting to tingle. Could Brooke

and Amaryllis be right? Could I learn to celebrate Selena again? How exactly did she fit into my history and the history of Texas?

I have decided to talk to Mom and Dad about this idea for Texas History Day. I don't want to tell them why I am worried about showing people how much Selena means to me.

When I asked to be called *Strella, I just told them I wanted to try something new for middle school. And because my parents are my parents, they were cool with it. I didn't tell them that it was because I felt I could never live up to the name they gave me.

*Strella

## Sunday, October 16, 2022

When I went to grab some pickle juice from the kitchen today (don't judge!), it made me remember the last time I was doing this very same thing a couple months ago. I was being extra quiet because we had only been living at Grandpa Raul's for a few weeks, and the kitchen is right next to his library.

He always makes me feel like I am too noisy or too American, or just *too much* in general, so I try really hard to stay out of his way. I was sneaking past when I noticed my dad standing in the doorway to the library.

"Why doesn't she speak more Spanish?" I heard Grandpa Raul ask, except it didn't sound like a question. More like he was barking an order. (I knew "she" must be me since Mom's Spanish is perfect.)

I didn't hear what Dad said, but then I heard Grandpa Raul reply, "Well, it's what your mother would have wanted."

My Grandma Santos? Why would she care if I spoke Spanish or not?

Dad nodded and started to close the door to the library. That's when I hid under the kitchen table so I wouldn't get caught eavesdropping.

I remember I had a sour taste in my mouth, and it wasn't from the pickle juice.

*Strella

## Thursday, October 20, 2022

Miss Diaz says we must have our topics narrowed down by November because that's when we will officially begin research. She gave us each a packet of information about Texas History Day to bring home.

Brooke and Amaryllis are so excited, and I am trying to be excited too. We decided we will spend the weekend doing internet research. Then on Monday, we will share what we find with each other.

*Strella


P.S. Mom asked me what I wanted to be for Halloween, and I said, "Not Selena." I thought she looked a little hurt since we always work on my costume together or have a family costume. She asked what I was thinking of doing instead, but I just shrugged. I'm not sure about anything, lately. Maybe my costume should be a big question mark.

## Monday, October 24, 2022

When I got to Miss Diaz's class, Brooke and Amaryllis couldn't wait to share what they'd learned about Selena.

We watched video clips of Selena. We looked at memes and tons of pictures of all Selena's fans—old and young—who still love her. We looked at lots of websites, including one for a museum dedicated to Selena. It's in Corpus Christi, a couple hours away, and of course my mom and I have been there!

So I told Brooke and Amaryllis about the time we went there.

The museum was amazing, but at one point, Mom made me close my eyes. I was too excited to be embarrassed, so I closed my eyes and let her lead me.

When she told me to open my eyes, we were right in front of one of *Selena's actual costumes.*

Her costumes were one of the things she was most known for. This one had a white sparkly bustier and tight white pants. (In case you don't know, a bustier is basically a tight top that kind of looks like a bedazzled swimsuit! Selena wore them a lot when she performed.) Without thinking, I touched the case. It was one thing to see pictures of Selena's costumes, but to see something she wore in person made her feel more real to me than she ever had before.

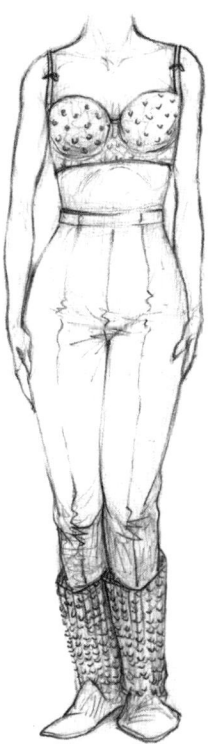

Everything we looked at this morning reminded me why my parents loved Selena so much and brought up all the memories and traditions we have formed around her.

Seeing Brooke and Amaryllis's excitement as they discover this whole world of Selena makes my heart hurt a little bit. I wish she were still alive. She was someone Mexican Americans were so proud of. She was special, and she was taken away.

But when I watch videos of Selena talking or telling jokes in interviews, I feel happy because she sounds like me when I speak! She tried her best with Spanish, but she wasn't perfect. For example, I know Selena struggled with rolling her r's correctly and remembering certain words in Spanish. But because she tried, people—even people in Mexico—seemed to accept her as she was.

Selena was determined to keep working on her Spanish, and so am I. Maybe that will make Grandpa Raul like me more.

Part of me wishes I had never overheard Grandpa Raul say that my Spanish isn't very good. And the other part of me wishes he could see how hard I am trying to fit in—in his house, in my new school, and in this in-between world of Spanish and English.

Is there a chance he can ever accept me just as I am—as just *Strella?

"Earth to *Strella," I heard Brooke say, and I laughed.

They asked if I knew how to do any of Selena's dances. Too bad we aren't in our old house in San Antonio. I could invite them over to watch the Selena movie and dance to her music. But I don't want to do that at Grandpa Raul's. I can just imagine what he would say about all the noise we'd make.

*Strella

## Monday, October 31, 2022

The decision has been made. I am going trick-or-treating as a question mark. It was sort of a joke at first, but now I think it's the perfect idea.

I don't know if Mom and Dad agree with me, but they bought me some glittery poster board anyway. Like I said before, they're cool like that.

I have some cutting and gluing to do even though I'm pretty MEH at crafts. Just like most other things.

*Strella the ?

That's me.

## Tuesday, November 1, 2022

Dad is always the most quiet on this day. It's Grandma Santos's birthday. It's also All Saints' Day. That's why Grandma's parents named her Santos. *Santo* is saint in Spanish.

I found my dad in the music room, and I asked if he would mind playing those Lydia Mendoza songs. I thought maybe the music would help him share more of his memories about Grandma Santos. I know he loved her so much.

Dad patted the spot on the floor next to him. Grandma Santos had an old-fashioned record player in the corner of the room. It sat on a small cabinet that was filled with her favorite records.

Dad pulled one out and asked if I could read the Spanish words on the record sleeve. I traced my finger over the picture and read out loud: "Lydia Mendoza y su guitarra de oro." I felt the Spanish roll around on my tongue, and my brain working hard to understand it. I asked Dad if it was "Lydia Mendoza and her guitar of gold."

He nodded and pointed to the smaller letters in the corner that read "La alondra de la frontera." This one was harder. I asked Dad what an alondra was. He said that alondra is a songbird, and frontera is the border. It means places like El Paso that share a border with Mexico.

He slid the record out of its sleeve and gently placed it on the record player. I love the scratchy sound a record makes when it begins to play.

Soon Lydia's voice filled the air. My dad sat back down, cross-legged on the floor next to me, and we just listened.

Out of the corner of my eye, I thought I saw Grandpa Raul lurking near the doorway. But the music drew me back in. I tried to remember what Grandma Santos's voice sounded like. I tried to imagine a version of Grandpa who loved to listen to her sing, and what it would be like to have a musical gift to share with people. Or any gift at all.

"Y'know, *Strella," Dad said when the music came to a stop, "some people call Lydia Mendoza the Mother of Tejano Music."

Wait, WHAT?

Dad laughed and told me not to worry—that Selena did her own thing and would always be the "Queen." He explained that Selena took traditional Tejano sounds that blended Mexican music with German and Czech sounds like the accordion and then added pop elements. "Did you know she unseated Laura Canales, who dominated the Tejano music scene in the '80s?" he asked.

I didn't even know who Laura Canales was. My dad nerds out like this sometimes, but I love hearing him talk about something he loves. Then, Dad asked me to grab his laptop because he wanted to show me a website where I could hear more Mexican and Mexican American music if I wanted.

I asked Dad for a sticky note and wrote down *Smithsonian Folkways Recordings* to Google later. This had to be the same Smithsonian Miss Diaz talked about in class, with the new museum. Cosmic connection!

I realize I've got so much more to learn about the world of music!

*Strella

## Saturday, November 5, 2022

I asked my mom why Grandpa Raul insists on speaking Spanish to me even though he understands English just fine. Does he know that I'm only in Spanish level 1 at school? Sometimes it seems that he's trying to frustrate me more than help me learn.

Mom said Grandpa Raul can be "old school" and that speaking Spanish can be a sign of respect for one's elders and honoring our roots. Then she made the ultimate Mom move. "What if you just tried speaking with your Grandpa Raul, *Strella?" she said. "Try starting a conversation."

I told her I didn't want to have a conversation. Then I just started saying everything in my head: "I feel like Grandpa Raul thinks I'm too American or something! I heard him tell Dad that my Spanish is bad. Why would I want to practice with him when he is grouchy all the time? He doesn't care about who I am or who Gabbo is—and *everyone* loves Gabbo. And I AM trying to learn Spanish, remember?!"

I don't know who was more shocked, me or Mom.

Mom and Dad had been tiptoeing around Grandpa Raul because he was "recovering." But when I stormed off, I made sure to slam the door to my room, just to make it clear that I was tired of "tiptoeing."

I had hoped that once Grandpa Raul was feeling better he might appreciate everything Mom and Dad were doing to help. I wanted him to see how much we were trying to be a part of his life. But he spends all his time in his library, alone. Even though we are just rooms away from one another, it feels like we might as well have the whole state of Texas between us.

Why did we even come here?

*Strella

## Thursday, November 10, 2022

Turns out Miss Diaz is also a huge Selena fan like my mom and like I used to be (or still am in secret). When Brooke, Amaryllis, and I told her that we were now officially going to move forward with "Selena's Triumph and Tragedy" as our topic, Miss Diaz was the one to jump out of her chair with excitement.

BUT, we have a lot of work to do. When you participate in History Day, there are a lot of different types of projects you can choose from. We decided not to write a paper because that would be hard to do as a team. We thought about creating a website, but after Brooke found so many Selena websites, we didn't know what more we could offer than they already had. So we decided to talk to Miss Diaz.

Amaryllis would love to do a performance because she wants to be an actress. Brooke—like me—loves to write, and we thought between the three of us we could put a script together. I'm not sure what kind of actress I am, but I'm just going to guess that I'm not a very good one based on my singing ability. I like to tell a story with words but not so much with my body, like an actor or performer does.

Miss Diaz asked what we thought about the documentary option. We could still do some writing, she said. Amaryllis could still do some acting. Then, we could learn how to put together all the videos and memes and information we found to tell the story of Selena's triumphs throughout her life and career.

"You're a genius, Miss Diaz!" I said.

Then Miss Diaz suggested that we might need something more to wow our audience. She tapped her pen against her chin, which she always does when she's thinking. "I've got it!" she said. "Oral histories."

An oral history is when you interview someone in order to record their story to share with others, or something like that. Miss Diaz said we could ask people what Selena meant to them, and what it is like now that she is a star sparkling above us. (That's what I like to believe she is anyway.)

Brooke, Amaryllis, and I grinned at each other as Miss Diaz handed us an oral history guide from the Smithsonian Institution. She explained that these oral histories, or interviews, would help us learn about how the past affects the present.

We went back to our Team Table to look through the parts Miss Diaz highlighted for us. We took notes on what to do before, during, and after the interviews. We made a list of equipment we would need, and most importantly, people we could interview. At the top of the list are my mom and dad. I'm hoping my mom will let us look through all the Selena stuff she has. My dad can fill us in on the history of Tejano music.

But that's where the list stopped.

Then Brooke looked at me and said we were forgetting one very important person.

"Who?" I asked.

She pointed at me. Amaryllis nodded and said, "*Strella, you need to share *your* story too."

## Sunday, November 13, 2022

I took some time to think about Brooke and Amaryllis's idea.

At dinner tonight, I told everyone about our plans. Grandpa Raul had the usual judgy look on his face as I explained it.

Gabbo added, "Don't expect to interview me."

Before I could snap back at Gabbo, Grandpa Raul, out of the blue, said that Tejanos have a complicated history.

I've never been at a quieter table in MY LIFE as we all stared at Grandpa Raul. During our meals, he usually just says things in Spanish like, "The meat needs more salt."

Grandpa Raul slowly folded his dinner napkin and placed it on the center of his scraped-clean plate. "Life," he began, "was especially hard for people with Mexican roots in Texas—and still can be."

He said that the history of Texas and Tejanos is tied to the history of Northern Mexico. He said that a lot of the land that makes up the United States today was once a part of Mexico. Part of that was due to the Treaty of Guadalupe Hidalgo, which officially ended the Mexican-American War. But Mexicans who stayed in the U.S. after that lost many of the rights that had been promised to them. "Including the right to speak Spanish freely," Grandpa Raul said.

The rice I was chewing nearly got stuck in my throat.

Then Grandpa Raul told us that when he was in the Vietnam War, people still said mean things to him about where he was from and how he spoke. He didn't have a sense of pride, or *orgullo*, in being a Tejano then. He wanted to be accepted as American, not "Mexican American."

Because of this, Grandpa Raul didn't want his kids to speak Spanish.

As I listened to him, I was reminded of something I'd learned about Selena's family while I was researching—that her father felt the same way and wanted his kids to be American. Grandpa Raul thought speaking English instead of Spanish would help his children be more accepted. And maybe that is why Selena struggled with Spanish, because her father had discouraged it.

But now Grandpa Raul knows differently, he said. He doesn't want us to ever be ashamed of our Spanish language, or to lose it.

I thought he was getting off track, but then, get this: He looked AT ME and said he'd heard my outburst last weekend. He hadn't meant to hurt my feelings, but he wanted to do more for me and Gabbo than he had for Dad and my tías and tíos.

He made the mistake of not listening to Grandma Santos about how important Spanish is, and he wants to fix it now. He wants all of us to take pride in being able to speak the language of our culture and history.

It gets even better—and more unbelievable!

Grandpa told me he was proud of how hard I've been working on this project and on my Spanish. He said if I ever needed help, I could find him in his library. Then, he excused himself from the table.

Maybe at last I'm beginning to see what's behind Grandpa Raul's storm clouds.

*Strella

## Thursday, November 17, 2022

Miss Diaz told us that there will be a Hullabaloo on Saturday at the El Paso Public Library.

Hullabaloo is a strange word that just means a chance for us to meet with a librarian for help with our research. There will also be other History Day volunteers who can help us with different parts of our project, like the thesis statement or how to organize all our information. More than anything, I'd like to see other documentary film projects to inspire us.

Can I say that Brooke, Amaryllis, and I are just a teeny bit worried? The documentary is supposed to be like a mini-movie, and even though we've all used computers to edit clips from the internet to make funny little videos, none of us has made a *film*.

And we're not just showing who Selena was but also trying to get our audience to understand *why* she was so important to Tejano culture, and why she remains the Queen of Tejano Music today. Easy, right?

Not!

*Strella

## Saturday, November 19, 2022

You won't believe what happened.

Amaryllis's dad was going to pick us all up for the Hullabaloo, but their car had a flat tire. Brooke's mom was busy with Brooke's sisters, and my parents were out on a hike in the Franklin Mountains with Gabbo.

Did you ever hear of that saying, "Desperate times call for desperate measures"? Well, this was one of them.

There was only one person who could help us: Grandpa Raul. He still had a car, though I hardly ever saw him drive it.

I straightened my spine, pulled my shoulders back, and took a deep breath. Then, I knocked on his library door.

"Adelante," he said, which meant I could enter.

"Grandpa Raul, con permiso," I said, excusing myself, "pero tengo una problema."

Grandpa Raul peered at me over the top of his book for what seemed like a long while. Then he marked his place with a bookmark, closed the book, and set it on the armrest of his recliner.

"I see you're still practicing your Spanish," he said IN ENGLISH.

I nodded, confused.

"¿Cual es el problema?" he asked, switching back to Spanish.

"Me puedes llevar a mis amigas y a mí a la . . . library," I said slowly, trying to find the right words in the right order but then blanking on the word for library. I thought of the videos of Selena doing her best to speak in Spanish. I remembered how she wouldn't hide or be embarrassed. So I tried to do the same.

"Biblioteca," Grandpa Raul offered.

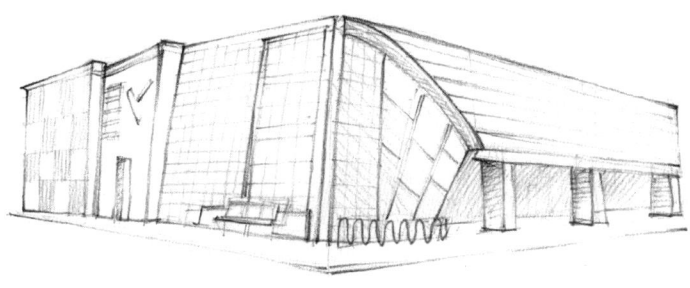

I nodded and laughed, embarrassed. To my surprise, he smiled.

Then he said in English that libraries were one of his favorite places. I told him me too! And then in a rush, I told him about the Hullabaloo and how important it was for us to get there.

"¡Pues, vámonos!" he said and slowly pushed himself up from the recliner. I wondered if his heart was healing the way it should. As if he could read my thoughts, he swatted at the air like there was a fly buzzing around him. "No te preocupes," he said. "Don't worry."

I decided to listen.

The Hullabaloo was SO FUN, and the librarian that we met with LOVED our project idea. She suggested we create something called a storyboard, so we're planning to do that after Thanksgiving. Grandpa Raul stayed the whole time. He listened and even asked some helpful questions.

As we were leaving the library, I said "Gracias, Grandpa Raul."

He said he was happy to be here with me, and if I wanted, he could help with the project—as long as it wasn't any of the fancy technical stuff.

I was completely surprised, and also overwhelmed with thankfulness.

*Strella

### Saturday, December 3, 2022

Brooke and Amaryllis came over today. This is the first time I've had friends visit since we moved to El Paso. (Wow—I just realized that Brooke and Amaryllis have become my friends and aren't just my teammates anymore!)

It was a big day: Mom showed us what she calls her "Selena Archive." But when she came back from the storage unit with a big rubber container, I felt a little disappointed. *That* was the archive? I expected a beautiful box with bows and dried roses all over it.

But you shouldn't judge a box by its cover, because inside, it was AMAZING. Mom had saved even more than I knew. She told us when she worked at the Guadalupe Cultural Arts Center, she had learned how to preserve items so they don't fall apart over time. She had tons and tons of stuff—photos, T-shirts, concert tickets, posters, books, magazines, and lots more. The box even had melted candles from the vigils Mom attended after Selena died.

Brooke, Amaryllis, and I looked at each other. We knew THIS would be the perfect time to interview my mom and literally unpack history.

Brooke whipped out her phone, and I set it up on the tripod Dad bought us for the project. We adjusted it so that Mom appeared perfectly framed by all the Selena memorabilia she had saved.

"Mom, what is this?" I laughed as I held up what looked like a Selena-style bustier.

"That's what I was wearing when your dad and I met at Selena's concert in Houston!" she said with a wink.

We giggled and gathered around as Mom held the bustier up to her chest and did a little shoulder shake for us.

We had studied the oral history guide Miss Diaz had given us. It had some possible questions, but we wanted ones more related to our project. So then she suggested we look at the interview questions on one of the Smithsonian Learning Lab's resources. *Boom!* We found tons of stuff about music and memory.

I pulled out the list of questions we had jotted down, and we started our interview with Mom. After making her tell us her name—to be official!— we asked when she first heard Selena sing and if there was a special Selena song she holds in her heart.

Mom said she saw Selena on *The Johnny Canales Show*, sometime in the late 1980s. "Selena sang a lot about love," Mom said and paused. I swear she was blushing! She said if she had to pick an all-time favorite song it would be "Amor Prohibido." Mom's parents were worried about her marrying a musician (my dad!). Mom felt like she had a forbidden love like Selena sings about in that song. Selena knew about amor prohibido in her own life too.

Then, we asked her to tell us about all the stuff in her Selena Archive.

Each item she showed us brought up a different memory. Mom told us about concerts she went to, and about how she used to try to style her hair like Selena did. When she pulled out the last item, a CD of Selena's called *Ven Conmigo (Come with Me)* Mom decided it was time for a spontaneous dance party.

"I'm going to teach you to dance a cumbia!" she said. Brooke and Amaryllis looked at me and grinned.

I ran to the music room and grabbed Dad's old boom box. Mom popped the CD in and pushed play.

A quick "Hey" came out of the speakers along with an upbeat tempo, and Mom sang along to the music.

"*Nadie se quede sentado. Todos vamos a bailar.*"

"Come on, girls! Baila, baila!" Mom shouted. "Selena says, 'No one stays seated—everyone go dance!'" She shook her hips to the music and grabbed my arm to spin me. I spun so fast the world became a blur of colors. Amaryllis and Brooke joined in.

"Play it again!" we shouted when the song ended.

Mom hit repeat, and we danced until we couldn't breathe. Also, we forgot to turn the camera off. But by then, we already had an audience of Dad, Gabbo, and Grandpa Raul.

I don't know if I'm imagining it, but Grandpa Raul's house is feeling different. Maybe it's Selena's spirit that is helping lift all of us up and turning this house into our home.

*Strella

## Sunday, December 4, 2022, Mom's Interview

I had time this afternoon to watch our video from yesterday. I wrote down word for word what Mom said. Here are some of my favorite parts:

*Selena worked tirelessly to achieve her dreams. To me, she is a symbol of creativity, drive, and love of family. She had wild success, yet she still lived in the neighborhood she grew up in. She was down to earth. The type of person who liked feeling the warm pavement beneath her feet, performed random acts of kindness for the neighborhood kids, and couldn't stop adopting pets.*

*Selena was a woman who turned the male-*

*dominated world of Tejano music upside down, and she didn't stop there ... When Selena opened Selena Etc., I was awed by her business sense. The boutique featured her fashion designs. Fancy clothes. Everyday clothes. It even had a hair and nail salon!*

*Like me, Selena was from a working-class family, and she valued education. I thought of her when I graduated from high school, when I graduated from college, and I know I will think of her again when I earn my master's degree. My dream is to run my own nonprofit for the arts, and I like to think I am honoring Selena's legacy by doing so.*

*Without her, I don't know if I would have dared to dream so big. Even now, I choose to keep shining bright like a star in the sky—that was her example and challenge to all of us.*

My mom always told me that Selena made her feel proud to be a Mexican American, and now I finally know what she means.

*Strella

## Monday, December 12, 2022

Brooke, Amaryllis, and I are still researching.

There's so much on the internet, it's kinda overwhelming. In a way, the archive Mom made is like a mini-internet from before there was the internet! In the past, you just had to be lucky enough to find articles in an actual magazine or catch a performance or interview on TV. Now, you just click a link to access information.

From my research I learned that the movie version and the streaming series did a pretty good job of capturing Selena's star power and who she was as a person—adventurous, playful, and willing to fight for what she wanted! She had CHARISMA.

Grandpa Raul took us back to the public library, and the librarian helped us find some books on Tejano music. For this part of the documentary, Brooke, Amaryllis, and I are also going to interview my dad. When it comes to music, his brain is like a Google search. Instead of typing a word or phrase into the search bar, all I have to do is ask him a question, and he has an answer.

*Strella

## Friday, December 16, 2022, Dad's Interview

Brooke, Amaryllis, and I watched some of Selena's performances from The Johnny Canales Show Mom mentioned. Selena was fire even then!

Then we agreed we needed to focus and went to Grandma Santos's music room to set up for my dad's interview. Here are a few highlights from what he said:

*What does Selena mean to me? Selena inspired me as a performer and musical artist. Girl could dance, but she also set a record for attendance at the Houston Astrodome—and that was incredibly important, because she was playing Tejano music before there was really stage time for us. There were all kinds of people at the concert, not just Tejanos or Mexican Americans or Latinos.*

*At that concert, she began with a disco medley before launching into her Spanish songs, and it just showed how skilled she was in moving between genres of music. She reminds me to take all the music I love and create my own sound.*

*She died right before the crossover of her music into the English market. Her single "Dreaming of You" became a hit. Selena was part of the wave in the '90s that became known as the "Latin explosion." She paved the way for so many artists—not just Latino artists. Her music lifted people up, and her performances inspired.*

We also learned from Dad that by the time Selena was fifteen, she had appeared on the cover of *Tejano Entertainer* magazine and was nominated for Female Vocalist of the Year at the Tejano Music Awards. I could fill pages with the list of awards she's won. And in

2022, she was given a star on the Hollywood Walk of Fame.

I love that. A star—the perfect symbol for Selena.

*Strella

## Wednesday, December 28, 2022

I was really hoping to get my own cell phone for Christmas. I think almost twelve is old enough, don't you? But I got something way more special. Grandpa Raul gave me a charm bracelet. It's so beautiful. It only has one charm on it so far—a book—but he said that we can keep adding charms to celebrate special moments or events.

I'm not sure what's different with Grandpa Raul, but he seems less angry now.

Maybe I am too?

*Strella

Monday, January 9, 2023

---

Happy New Year! We are back in our escuela! I'm probably the only person excited for school again, based on all the bummed faces I saw around me.

I like Spanish class and Language Arts, but Social Studies with Miss Diaz is still my favorite. I'm learning so much about the history of Texas, the history of Mexican Americans, and even the history of me. (Thank you, Miss Diaz!)

I am still happy I chose *Strella for myself this school year, but I also am getting back to liking being named after the Queen of Tejano Music. It feels like a gift.

My mom and I karaoked to a lot of Selena songs over the holiday break, and even though my singing has NOT improved, my Spanish has. (Go ahead and ask me to roll my r's!)

I will tell you that one thing I know about Spanish is that sometimes I'll hear something in a song or something someone says, and I know deep in my gut that Spanish is the best way to say it. You can translate it into other languages, but sometimes you can only capture the exact meaning in its original language.

*Strella

## Tuesday, February 7, 2023

Miss Diaz said to try to keep on recording the details of our lives, but it's been hard to find time with school and our History Day project and everything else.

Brooke, Amaryllis, and I did a fun thing where we set up a Selena booth outside of the grocery store. My mom said we could do a few of these "pop-ups" to interview people in our area. Getting a bunch of opinions and information from all kinds of people is called crowdsourcing, and we're gonna need a CROWD to get this documentary done!

It's been fun because even though they are being recorded, most people haven't been too shy. They want to talk about what makes Selena special to them. Mom got this idea from a show she listens to on National Public Radio called *StoryCorps*. They have a little recording studio in a trailer where people can go and share their own personal story.

I am learning that we all have stories to tell.

So far, one thing is clear: People love Selena because she was real. And maybe that's why Mom loves her so much too, because I know my mom never pretends to be anyone she is not.

I realize now that just because Selena and I share a name doesn't mean I have to be just like her (like I was trying to do in elementary school). It's okay if I'm not a great singer or super musical. I can still *love* music.

And it's okay if I'm still learning about my own gifts as a person. I just need to make the most of them as I discover them.

All school year, I've been showing up as *Strella, and I've made two of my best friends ever because of it.

*Strella

# Friday, February 17, 2023

We had the school-wide Feedback Fair for History Day today. I didn't mention it because I was FREAKING OUT.

Miss Diaz had said it was okay for us to just show our storyboard. Thanks to the Hullabaloo, the storyboard helped us organize all the information we collected. It also helped us think about how the interviews were a part of the "big picture" for the project.

Brooke, Amaryllis, and I put in A LOT of hours on the storyboard, and I am proud of us.

A storyboard is kind of like a map or chart that shows your plan. On ours, the left side shows copies of the headlines from the newspaper clippings about Selena—not just about the tragedy, but also about the triumph of Selena's amazing impact during her life. The right side of the storyboard highlights interview quotes that show Selena's legacy through the generations. (Bonus vocab points!)

When Gabbo saw it, he said, "It doesn't look horrible." If you have a big brother, then you know that this is as close as you get to a compliment.

But I was still nervous. It's more than a little scary for me to think about sharing our work with an audience—especially at school. It's like being on stage, which is not my favorite place to be, as you know. But then I remembered a scene in the *Selena* movie where Selena is sitting on the roof and looking up at the moon. Suzette, Selena's sister, asks her what's she doing, and Selena says she's "dreaming" of all she can be.

So last night, I looked up at the night sky, picked a star, and wished for everyone to see all the hard work we've put into planning for our documentary about Selena.

Maybe dreaming and wishing and working hard all sort of come together, because everyone loved our storyboard!

*Strella

## Monday, February 20, 2023

Now that we received our feedback from the fair, Miss Diaz said we can FINALLY begin to put together our real-life documentary: Selena's Triumph and Tragedy.

Our documentary only has to be 10 minutes long, but we've got SO MUCH material to work with. That's one question teachers and students had for us: How are we going to decide what to include and what to leave out?

Do I wish now that we had made an "exhibit" instead of a documentary for the competition instead? Maybe. But you know who wanted to learn more about documentaries after the Hullabaloo? Grandpa Raul. Neat, right?

Because Brooke, Amaryllis, and I have to do the work ourselves, Dad and Grandpa Raul just watch and bring us snacks as we clip video and audio and images. It takes hours and hours to edit and then stitch them all together in a way that makes sense. It's like a big puzzle, but we get to decide what the final picture will be.

Today, we decided who would narrate for us. We chose Amaryllis because she has the most dramatic flair!

*Strella

## Saturday, March 18, 2023

History Day contest season is officially here, and our documentary is done! It took most of spring break and LOTS of weekends, but WE DID IT!

The coolest (and hardest) thing to make was the opening. It starts with a video of Selena singing and dancing when she was our age. She quickly begins to morph into the star we know and love today. (And, yes, that took us a LOOOOOONG time to figure out how to do!) Then, newspaper and magazine headlines about her death take over the screen.

We set the whole opening to "Como La Flor," but the music fades into silence when we come to the tragedy. The silence then becomes a blur of voices from the oral histories we collected before we cut to a picture of Mom at a vigil for Selena.

Mom's interview is the first oral history in the documentary, because she shares her Selena Archive. Brooke, Amaryllis, and I thought it would be good for our audience to know the facts about Selena's life, but also hear firsthand about how she changed the lives of regular people.

From there, the documentary moves back and forth between the interviews, and Amaryllis narrating about important events and achievements. Then at the end, it shows all of us dancing and laughing and singing along to Selena's music in Grandpa Raul's dining room—our dining room!

Not to brag, but I think this is a case of "you need to see it to believe it!" That's how amazing our documentary turned out!

\*Strella

## Saturday, March 25, 2023

Do you know what we had to do at Regionals today? Say our names. THAT'S IT! Okay, we said our names AND the title of our documentary.

A History Day volunteer had our documentary ready to "screen" for the judges, so we just stepped aside as the lights dimmed and our documentary began to play. Brooke, Amaryllis, and I held hands and tried not to giggle from the butterflies tickling our stomachs. We watched the judges' faces for signs, hoping they loved it.

I wonder if there are enough stars in the sky for me to wish on tonight, because I am dreaming of Washington, D.C.!

*Strella

## Sunday, April 16, 2023

Happy Selena Day!!! (And happy birthday to me!) The familia and Brooke and Amaryllis surprised me with a party today! They had my favorite kind of chocolate cake and Neapolitan ice cream on the side. Three flavors in one—YUM.

As happy as I was, I kind of missed the white roses, purple and black streamers, and pizza that we used to always have for my Selena-themed birthday parties.

But all of us had something to celebrate, because—drum roll... **WE LEARNED THAT OUR DOCUMENTARY WAS SELECTED FOR THE STATE COMPETITION!**

Friday, May 5, 2023

I am writing this morning because I'm so nervous about the History Day State Competition today. Everyone's coming—Mom, Dad, Grandpa Raul, and even Gabbo.

We'll be at UTEP, which is the University of Texas here in El Paso. I've been to the campus with Mom when she was applying to graduate school last summer. She's been taking classes on top of helping Grandpa Raul and our family and me with my project. If Mom can get through all that, I can get through this day.

Sí se puede!

*Strella

Saturday, May 6, 2023

# PINCH ME.

We did it. We're going to Washington, D.C.!!

## Sunday, June 11, 2023

Can you believe I have never been on a plane? In my family, we always drive everywhere. We are now at the University of Maryland in a city called College Park. It was such an adventure getting here!

When Dad, Grandpa Raul, and Gabbo dropped Mom and me off at the airport this morning, there were tears. Not from me or Mom or Gabbo, who was mainly just jealous that I was going on a big trip. But Dad had tears (he always has BIG feelings) and even Grandpa Raul did. He said again that he was PROUD OF ME. I wished that they could all come along—even Gabbo.

The air at the airport had too many smells. None of them familiar to me—like the smell of Grandpa Raul's library or the smell of the desert after it rains. Those smells I find comforting now more than ever.

On the bright side, Mom offered me the seat by the window so I could see El Paso grow smaller and smaller as we flew higher and higher. Soon we were sailing in a sea of clouds.

When we landed in D.C., everyone clapped, and I got to say "Thank you" to the captain as we got off the plane. The D.C. airport had the same smell as the Chicago and El Paso airports, but I noticed one difference: Not as many people here look like me and Mom as they do in El Paso.

Now we are in our hotel and getting ready for bed. We spent the whole day traveling, but I am still not tired. We'll here for about a week, and Mom said she has a few surprises planned. How will I ever fall asleep?

*Strella

## Monday, June 12, 2023

The campus is WOW. Today we had a tour and then went to a giant picnic at McKeldin Mall. It's not like a mall where you go shopping. Imagine something like a football field with sidewalks that lead to a spectacular fountain. I laughed (but also wanted to hide) when Mom took off her shoes and started dancing a cumbia in the water. She tried to get me to join her, but I waited for her on the grass.

Brooke and Amaryllis and their parents met us at a building with giant pillars like you would see in ancient Greece. They were easy to spot, even with so many other History Day students running around. We all wore matching "Anything for Selenas" tie-dyed shirts. Together, we went to find Miss Diaz and surprised her with a Selena T-shirt too. Miss Diaz hugged the T-shirt and then put it on right over her dress.

Miss Diaz shared that we will present our documentary at the Smithsonian National Museum of American History on Thursday. Isn't that AMAZING? Like before, we just introduce ourselves, say the name of our documentary, and then stand by with our butterfly stomachs while our video plays.

There will even be a live webcast of the event, so everyone in my family can stream the ceremony. You'd think I'd be more nervous, but all of this is already more than I ever dreamed. And like Selena said, "Always believe that the impossible is always possible."

*Strella

## Tuesday, June 13, 2023

Mom and I went on a city adventure. The first stop was Jumbo Slice Pizza Mart for lunch. The pizza slice was nearly the size of my torso! I'm not even exaggerating. Mom took a picture to show Gabbo later how enormous it was (and to capture it dripping with cheesy goodness). You might think I shared my slice with Mom, but I managed to eat it all on my own.

You can guess what happened next. I begged her to go back to the hotel so I could lie down and recover from overeating. She said we should "walk it off" instead. I think she wanted to squeeze in a few more of her surprises.

Our next stop was a bookstore with a restaurant in it! I admit I raised my eyebrows at Mom because there was NO WAY I could fit more food in this body. But she said we weren't there to eat. We were going to "browse, buy, and spy." She told me that one of the things she likes about this store is that they "hold space" for people to talk about hard things going on in our society. A lot of the books on their shelves showcase authors who are writing about important issues. Mom was thinking about ideas for the arts center she hopes to open in El Paso after she graduates.

Mom wasn't the only person who left inspired. I hadn't thought about writing as a way to create change in the world, but now I am.

*Strella

## Wednesday, June 14, 2023

Mom's surprises continue. Today we left campus and took a ride to Union Station on the Metro. I never knew a train station could be beautiful! Union Station has rows of white arches that feel as big as a rainbow's, and everything seems to be lined with gold. I love how everything echoes—our voices, our shoes hitting the ground, our laughter. It was awesome.

Then Brooke and Amaryllis and their parents joined us for a tour where you hop on and off a bus at different famous sites around the city. We took so many pictures—of the Vietnam Memorial for Grandpa Raul, the Martin Luther King Jr. Memorial, the White House, the Library of Congress, and my favorite, the Lincoln Memorial.

There were so many things to see that we only had time to grab some (normal-sized) pizza for dinner. Then we all came back and collapsed at the hotel. We have to rest up for our big day tomorrow!

*Strella

## Friday, June 16, 2023

OMGOMGOMG!!!!

Yesterday was so busy, I didn't have a chance to write. But let me set the scene for you . . .

The ceremony took place in the sports arena. Before it started, we were invited to join in a parade on the court. Students were waving flags from Texas to Minnesota and from California to Tennessee. Some students wore hats that looked like blocks of cheese and held up signs that read "Wisconsin Proud." There were blow-up cows, lobsters, dinosaurs, and even a pirate. I saw students waving sunflowers, chili peppers, and all sorts of other stuff.

It was so fun! Brooke, Amaryllis, and I walked and waved along with everyone else, proudly wearing our Selena T's.

After we took our seats in the bleachers, the "champion of history and history students," Dr. Cathy Gorn, was introduced. She thanked everyone who had made this History Day celebration possible, and she congratulated all the students and hoped that we would remain lifelong learners. She told us to give a round of applause for our parents because we wouldn't be here without them.

I reached for Mom's hand and squeezed it. I realized this year that I wouldn't be who I am without my parents, without my family, without my friends, and without Selena.

I was lost in thought when I heard Dr. Gorn say she would no longer keep us in suspense. She began with the paper category and announced the winners for the junior and senior age groups. I watched student after student proudly cross the stage to collect their medal.

Finally, it was time for the documentary category. Miss Diaz, Brooke, Amaryllis, Mom, and I all held hands as the names for the bronze medal were called, then the silver, and finally ... the gold.

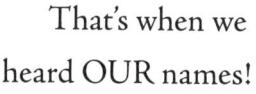

That's when we heard OUR names! You heard that right: We won! We won! We WON! We were pretty shocked, but that didn't stop Miss Diaz from jumping up and down and screaming with excitement. I think she would have raced us to the stage if teachers were allowed up there.

When Brooke, Amaryllis, and I were on the stage together, I could almost imagine how Selena must have felt under the bright lights. Feeling proud of your talents, proud of your culture, proud of yourself. You can get used to a feeling like that!

*Strella

## Saturday, June 17, 2023

For Mom's final surprise, we went to the Molina Family Latino Gallery. It's the first exhibit of the new National Museum of the American Latino. (The actual museum Miss Diaz mentioned when we first started this project!)

"This museum is all about people like us," I whispered to Mom as we walked in. Awe is one of the few things that can make me quiet.

The gallery is divided into sections, each dedicated to a different part of Latino history. We made our way through the ¡Presente! exhibit inside. I felt like Dad with his BIG FEELINGS. There was so much that reminded me of Texas and my family—pictures of people who looked like us, stories about people with my same heritage. And I realized that our house in El Paso now felt like "home." I'm not quite sure when that happened.

Next we went to the Somos Theater in the gallery. Mom said that *Somos* was also a documentary of sorts made especially for the theater. Alberto Ferreras (almost like Herrera!) used video interviews just like we did for our documentary. Watching it, I learned there are as many different ways of being Latino as there are stars in the sky.

Mom, who is basically a mind reader, asked if I remembered why they chose Estrella as part of my name. I looked at her, waiting to hear the story.

She pushed the hair away from my eyes and said, "I knew you would be a star who would shine brightly in your own way. Just look at where your light has led all of us."

Then she told me a cool fact: Even after a star dies, its light keeps traveling for a long time. So we see the light of the past in the present.

She said that my history project will help Selena's light continue to shine today and into the future. "You are part of her cultural legacy, and she is part of yours. I wanted to show you how connected your stories are—and to know that you have your own light to shine as well," she said. I gave her a big hug.

Then she handed me something that Grandpa Raul had asked her to give me. I unwrapped the small box. Inside was a new charm for my bracelet: a microphone. He included a little note that read "Use your voice to tell your story."

I swallowed hard because I could feel myself about to cry. Mom took the charm and added it to my bracelet. Then, hand in hand, we walked out of the museum.

Siempre,

Selena Estrella (*Strella) Herrera

# Select Glossary of Terms
## Spanish

**adelante** (ah-deh-lahn-teh): forward; come in

**alondra** (ah-lon-drah): songbird

**amiga** (ah-mee-gah): female friend

**amor** (ah-mohr): love

**bailar** (bye-lar): to dance

**biblioteca** (bib-lee-oh-tek-ah): library

**cantina** (can-teen-ah): bar or restaurant

**con permiso** (kohn per-mee-soh): excuse me

**cumbia** (koom-byah): a type of music and a dance similar to salsa

**escuela** (ehs-kweh-lah): school

**familia** (fah-mee-lee-ah): family

**frontera** (frohn-teh-rah): border

**gracias** (grah-see-ahs): thank you

**guitarra** (gee-tarr-ah): guitar

**llevar** (yeh-var): to take or carry

**no te preocupes** (no teh preh-oh-ku-pes): don't worry

**orgullo** (or-goo-yoh): pride

**oro** (or-oh): gold

**palabra** (pah-lah-brah): word

**problema** (pro-bleh-mah): problem

**prohibido** (pro-he-be-doh): forbidden

**sí se puede** (see se pweh-deh): yes, it is possible; yes we can

**siempre** (see-em-preh): always

**Tejano** (teh-hah-noh): a Texan of Hispanic descent; also, a popular type of music with Mexican and other influences

**tía** (tee-ah): aunt

**tío** (tee-oh): uncle

**vámonos** (bah-moh-nos): let's go

# English

**archive**: a collection of documents or information

**boutique**: a small shop that sells fashionable items

**charisma**: charm and likability

**documentary**: a presentation about factual events

**feedback**: opinions and suggestions provided after reviewing something

**generation**: people or family members from a similar period of time; children, parents, and grandparents are three different generations

**genre**: a category of music, art, or literature

**legacy**: something left or given by someone from the past

**lyrics**: words written to music

**male-dominated**: largely controlled by men

**medley**: a combination of songs

**memorabilia**: items that evoke memories and symbolize something

**narrate**: to provide voice or commentary

**nonprofit**: an organization with a goal other than making profit

**oral**: spoken

**prompt**: a suggestion to inspire a piece of writing

**script**: text written for a project or performance

**tragedy**: a sad event

**treaty**: an agreement

**tripod**: a three-legged stand

**triumph**: victory, success, or achievement

**Vietnam War**: a conflict fought in Southeast Asia from 1955 to 1975

# Discussion Questions

1. We meet Estrella at a point of transition. Not only did she have to move to a new city, she had to start at a new school. Did you ever have to start at a new school or move to a new city? What was that like for you? Does Estrella's story resonate with you?

2. Estrella works to learn Spanish to connect with Grandpa Raul. Have you been in a place where you did not understand the language spoken—either visiting a friend's house or visiting a new place? Did that experience make you want to learn more to connect?

3. As we know, Estrella's real first name is Selena. However, after an embarrassing situation at her old school, she wanted nothing to do with her old name. She took on her middle name and reinvented herself as *Strella. Have you done something or changed something to make yourself feel more comfortable in your identity?

4. Have you ever participated in History Day at your school? What kind of stories did you uncover as part of your research?

5. Estrella tells us about her visit to Washington, D.C., and the National Museum of the American Latino's Molina Family Latino Gallery. Have you been to the Smithsonian before? If you have not been able to visit Washington, D.C., what is your favorite museum in your local community? What is your favorite part of going to that museum?

6. Estrella and her friends' History Day project was about someone who inspired them, Selena Quintanilla-Pérez. Who inspires you and why?

# More Information

Selena Quintanilla-Pérez is known as the Queen of Tejano Music. Born in 1971, she grew up performing Tejano music with her Mexican American family around Texas at a young age. Her music grew Texan Mexican music audiences, contributing to a rise in the popularity of Latino music across the United States. She was the first Tejano music artist to win a Grammy Award in 1994 for her album, *Selena Live!* Selena's life ended tragically in 1995 after she was shot by the ex-manager of her fan club. A month after her passing, a final album was released, *Dreaming of You*. Selena then became the first music artist to have all (5) of her Spanish albums on the Billboard 200 at the same time.

Despite her early passing, Selena's memory and music continue to inspire Latina and Latino fans across different generations. Selena has been commemorated with a statue, a full-length film biopic, and a television series. She is even remembered by families who name their children after the famous singer, like we see with Estrella's family.

To find out more about Mexican American experiences, visit the free online Smithsonian Learning Lab Collection.

This QR code (when scanned using a phone app or a phone's camera) will bring you to the Smithsonian's Learning Lab, where Smithsonian Latino resources have been collected that relate to Tejano music, Selena Quintanilla-Pérez, and the Nuestras Voces series. You can also visit www.latino.si.edu for more information.

The Smithsonian has more than 154 million artifacts, works of art, and specimens in its collection. This includes everything from bugs to the space shuttle. These collections continue to grow.

Many of the Smithsonian's resources are available online. The digital Smithsonian effort includes making many of the collections searchable and available as primary source material.

# About the National Museum of the American Latino

The Smithsonian's National Museum of the American Latino advances the representation, understanding, and appreciation of Latino history and culture in the United States. The museum provides resources and collaborates with other museums to expand scholarly research, public programs, digital content, collections, and more. The museum operates its Molina Family Latino Gallery, the Smithsonian's first gallery dedicated to the Latino experience, at the National Museum of American History. Congress established the National Museum of the American Latino in 2020. Connect with the museum at latino.si.edu.

# Author's Note

As I was listening to the *Anything for Selena* podcast, I heard the testimonial of a fourteen-year-old content creator, Sonia Estrada, who was known around her school as the "Selena Girl." I recognized my own story in Sonia's because I too was a "Selena Girl"—not in 2021, but in 1995. Selena was instrumental in the development of my identity as a Mexican American (or in my Chicana Consciousness, as I referred to it then). When I was in tenth grade, my best friend Brooke, our friend Amy, and I participated in Minnesota History Day. We co-wrote and starred in a play that covered 500 years of Mexican American history titled *In the Course of the Sun*. While we never made it to Nationals like *Strella did, we did make it to State and enjoyed consolatory Dairy Queen blizzards afterward. History matters. Representation matters. I wanted to write this story for past, present, and future "Selena Girls," just like *Strella. Shine on and shine bright.

—V.R.

## About the Author

Vanessa Ramos was born in Texas and raised in Minnesota. She has dreamt about being many things: an astronomer, a paranormal investigator, a museum educator, an art historian, a curiosities curator, a paleontologist, and even an actress, but a writer is what she became. She holds an MFA in Creative Writing and an MA in Education from Hamline University. She has received awards, fellowships, and grants in support of her writing from the Texas Institute of Letters and The University of Texas, The Loft Literary Center and The Playwrights' Center in Minneapolis, and the Minnesota State Arts Board. She lives and teaches in the Twin Cities.

## About the Illustrator

Eugenia Nobati was born in Buenos Aires, where she still lives. She worked as a graphic designer before dedicating herself exclusively to illustration, drawing and painting everything from postage stamps and packaging to character design and animation backgrounds. Now specializing in illustration of children's books, her work has been published in nine countries and more than fifty books.

## Books in This Series